Terry and the Positivity

by Gabriela Henner!

Copyright © Gabriela Henner, 2019
ISBN: 9781709179518

I could not have finished this book without the immense amount of support I received from my family and friends. I am forever grateful for your love and kindness.

Dedicated to Sheila, my very own Positivity Pet.

one

Terry was a little monster with a big heart. He cooked meals for old monsters, he knitted scarves for the young ones, and he always said hello to every creature he met. Everyone knew him as the friendliest monster in town, skipping and singing everywhere he went.

three

Unfortunately, as time passed, he grew full of self-doubt and sadness.
He worried his singing was bad, he was too tired to skip,
and he stopped eating his tasty meals.

These unhappy feelings made him nervous around others,
and he felt more comfortable when alone.

His friends noticed this change in him and began to drift away,
only increasing his misery.

Terry became a thin and lonely monster.

five

One day, Terry went for a walk in the woods.
As he was admiring the tall trees and green grass,
an unexpected noise from behind startled him.
He turned around to see a little yellow pet seated on a log.

"Hello there! My name's Pep. I'm a Posi Pet!
Who are you?" the small monster asked.

"What's a Posi Pet? I'm just a regular monster, I guess," said Terry, sadly.

'A Posi Pet helps other monsters feel good about themselves by giving them compliments.
I don't think you're just any old monster. You're very polite,
and I've heard you can sing and skip really well!"

Terry felt a smile growing on his face, and noticed he didn't feel nervous
or worried around the golden pet.

They talked for hours and soon were best friends.

seven

After months of Pep's friendship and positive remarks,
Terry began to feel happier and more confident in himself.
He sang more often, and skipped every day in the woods with the little pet.

Terry realized he wanted to spend all of his time with the Posi Pet,
so he invited the small yellow monster to move in with him.
He even gave Pep his very own room!

nine

More time passed and a friend invited Terry to a New Year's Eve party.
Although the thought of so many monsters in one room scared him,
he knew Pep would be by his side, there to ease his fears.

As the day of the party drew nearer,
Terry became more excited and was ready to show everyone how much better he felt.
To celebrate his progress, the two monsters went out and bought bow ties!

eleven

Terry awoke on the morning of New Year's Eve, ready to have fun.
When he skipped into Pep's room to wake him up,
he discovered his best friend had fallen ill and lost his voice.

Oh no!

He nursed Pep all day with soup and hot tea, but nothing worked.
Terry would have to attend the party alone.

thirteen

He arrived late to the celebration, his stomach in knots.
Surrounded by so many monsters, all of the self-doubt and anxiety came rushing back.

What would they think of him?

What if they were mean to him?

How was he ever going to have fun when he felt so scared?

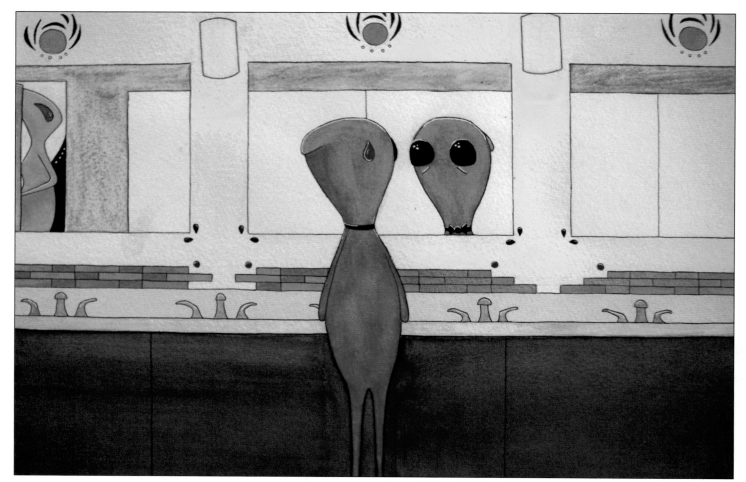

fifteen

He ran to the bathroom to calm down.
Terry tried to remember every nice remark Pep told him.
Then, he began to think of new, positive comments about himself
that no one had ever said to him.

When he realized this confidence and self-love had always been inside him,
a happiness bloomed in his heart!

seventeen

With newfound courage, he rushed back to the crowd and started dancing.
The other monsters noticed the old Terry had returned,
and suddenly he was the life of the party!

At the end of the night, a very happy Terry left for home.

He tiptoed into Pep's room and woke up his beloved friend.
Terry, giddy with excitement, told Pep about his success at the celebration.
The sleepy Posi Pet smiled and whispered, "I knew you'd find yourself.
That's the Terry I've known and loved all along."

nineteen

From that night on, Terry knew that he alone
had the power to make himself happy.

He and Pep continued to live together,
and they were an inseparable,
joyful pair of monsters.

Made in the USA
Lexington, KY
29 November 2019